Principal Sam and the Three Bears

by
Paul Semendinger, Ed.D.

Illustrated by
John Fredericks

PRINCIPAL SAM AND THE THREE BEARS

By Paul Semendinger, Ed.D.
Copyright © Paul Semendinger, Ed.D. 2018
Cover Copyright © John Fredericks 2018

Excelsior 1874 Books

Printed in the U.S.A.

ISBN-13: 978-1725625808
ISBN-10: 1725625806

To Laurie, Ryan, Alex, and Ethan, I love you! You are everything to me. Thanks, always, to my editor Britta Eastburg Friesen. Finally, special thanks to the wonderful students and staff of Hawes Elementary School who encourage me to be my best each and every day!

The sun was just beginning to rise over Principal Sam's house...

His eyes still full of sleep, Principal Sam squinted at his calendar and saw that it was **Read Across America Day.**

That woke him up! Today was the day the school librarian, Mrs. Travers, read fairy tales to the students. "I think I'll go and listen to them all!" Principal Sam said.

It had been a long time since Principal Sam listened to a fairy tale, but he loved all the silly characters like Little Red Riding Hood, the Gingerbread Man, and the Three Little Pigs.

While Principal Sam was greeting the students outside the school, Mrs. Travers rushed up to him. "We have an emergency!" she cried. "Someone misplaced all of the fairy tales in the library. I can't find them!"

Principal Sam thought, "Hmmm, I wonder if someone borrowed them and forgot to return them."

Then Principal Sam exclaimed, "I can help! I don't need the books. I know all those stories by heart."

After the opening bell and the flag salute, Principal Sam rushed to the library to meet the kindergarten class.

Principal Sam sat down in his special reading chair. He looked out at the children. "I am going to tell the story of Little Red Riding Hood," he said.

"Once upon a time there was a girl named Little Red Riding Hood. She traveled through a deep forest to visit her grandmother. On the way, she saw a trail of breadcrumbs and followed it until she reached a giant beanstalk."

"Little Red Riding Hood decided to climb the beanstalk all the way to the top. It went really high, reaching into the clouds."

"At the top, Little Red Riding Hood saw Jack and Jill. They had just fallen down a hill. Little Red Riding Hood took them to her grandmother's house where they got bandages and ate warm porridge.

The End."

15

When Principal Sam finished telling the story, all of the children applauded. Mrs. Travers said, "Principal Sam, that was good, but I think you mixed a few things up."

"Oh," said the principal, scratching his head. "I guess I was thinking of a different story."

"It's okay," the students called out. "We liked Principal Sam's story better than the real one!"

Soon a class of first grade students arrived to hear the story of the Gingerbread Man.

"Once upon a time there was a baker who made tasty treats. One day, as he took a sheet of gingerbread cookies out of the oven, one cookie jumped up and said, 'I want to run and run as fast as I can!'

"The baker said, 'You are fast! I will enter you in the town's race.'"

"The Gingerbread Man was set to race against a turtle and a rabbit. As he was running, the Gingerbread Man saw Little Miss Muffet eating her curds and whey."

"He sat down beside her and frightened Miss Muffet away. She ran so fast, she won the race!

The End."

The children clapped for this story too. Erin, a first grade student, said, "Principal Sam, that was a funny story, but I think you got mixed up."

"Hmm," said the principal, stroking his chin. "I guess I was thinking of a different story."

"That's okay," Erin and the children called out. "We liked your story better than the real one!"

Soon the second graders, the final class that morning, entered the library. They were ready to hear the story of the Three Bears.

"This is my favorite story!" said Principal Sam. "I love stories about bears!"

"Once upon a time there were three little bears. They were new to town and needed a place to live. They found some pigs who were selling their homes."

"The first pig had a house of straw. Papa Bear said, 'I don't want to live in a house of straw.' The second pig had a house of sticks. Mama Bear said, 'I don't want to live in a house of sticks.'"

"The third pig had a house of bricks. Baby Bear said, 'I like bricks. Can we live here?' Mama and Papa Bear said that the brick house was 'just right' and they moved in."

As the children were applauding the story, Mrs. Travers ran into the library. "I have the books, I have the books!" she exclaimed.

Principal Sam looked past the librarian. That's when he remembered that the books had been at his house the whole time!

Just then, a student named Auggie had a brilliant idea. "Since we have the books, we can now listen to the real stories!" he said.

"Yes," said Mrs. Travers. "I would love to read these stories to all the students!"

Principal Sam was feeling a little silly about forgetting to return the books and wanted to make it up to his students.

"How about this?" said Principal Sam. "We will have an assembly for the whole school. Mrs. Travers can read the real stories from the books to the whole school and the children can make decorations for the stage."

Soon the entire school was working together. The students and teachers were reading and writing, drawing and painting.

At the end of the school day, the students and teachers gathered in the auditorium. Mrs. Travers took out the first book and began reading the story, "Once upon a time there were three bears: Mama Bear, Papa Bear, and Baby Bear…"

And just like it says in the stories, "They all lived happily ever after…"

THE END

HOW TO DRAW THE BEAR!

STEP ONE:
Lightly sketch a circle.
(You'll erase some of these lines later)

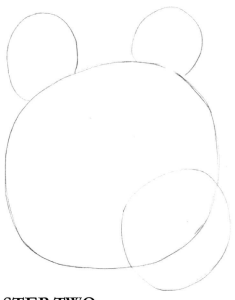

STEP TWO:
Add ears and a circle for the mouth area.

STEP THREE:
Add an oval for his nose, and some hair on top of his head.

STEP FOUR:
Draw some curves for his mouth, and a curve near his eyes.

<u>STEP FIVE:</u>
Add his eyes and mouth. Draw some jagged lines for his fur and his ears.

Trace over your final lines with pen or marker, and erase the pencil lines. Color him with crayons or colored pencils.

ABOUT THE AUTHOR

Dr. Paul Semendinger has been a teacher, educational speaker, and principal for almost thirty years. He is the author of *Principal Sam and the Calendar Confusion, Principal Sam Gets Fit* and *Impossible is an Illusion.* He's working on even more Principal Sam adventures and other children's works. Dr. Semendinger lives in New Jersey where he is the principal of the GREATEST elementary school in the whole world! You can follow Dr. Sem on Twitter **@DrPaulRSem**, and read his blog at: **www.drpaulsem.com**

ABOUT THE ILLUSTRATOR

John Fredericks has been drawing and painting since he could hold a pencil. (His mom's still mad about the marker on the wallpaper in Pottsville.) He has illustrated numerous roleplaying game products, and is a member of the Wyoming Valley Art League in Pennsylvania. You can follow him on Twitter and Instagram **@sketchingjohn**. He is also the author and illustrator of *Pegperson Pat*, available on Amazon and Kindle.

FOLLOW PRINCIPAL SAM!

Follow Principal Sam on Twitter at **@PrincipalSamBks**. There will be more books in this series, so be sure to look for them in the future.

Principal Sam loves to get mail from all his readers. You can e-mail him at principalsambooks@gmail.com. Send him your fan art, questions, and ideas. Principal Sam loves to hear from all his readers!

ALSO AVAILABLE:
Principal Sam and Calendar Confusion
Principal Sam Gets Fit

Made in the USA
Columbia, SC
08 January 2019